A Note to Parents and Teachers

Kids can imagine, kids can laugh and kids can learn to read with this exciting new series of first readers. Each book in the Kids Can Read series has been especially written, illustrated and designed for beginning readers. Humorous, easy-to-read stories, appealing characters, and engaging illustrations make for books that kids will want to read over and over again.

To make selecting a book easy for kids, parents and teachers, the Kids Can Read series offers three levels based on different reading abilities:

Level 1: Kids Can Start to Read

Short stories, simple sentences, easy vocabulary, lots of repetition and visual clues for kids just beginning to read.

Level 2: Kids Can Read with Help

Longer stories, varied sentences, increased vocabulary, some repetition and visual clues for kids who have some reading skills, but may need a little help.

Level 3: Kids Can Read Alone

Longer, more complex stories and sentences, more challenging vocabulary, language play, minimal repetition and visual clues for kids who are reading by themselves.

With the Kids Can Read series, kids can enter a new and exciting world of reading!

Franklin and the Contest

From an episode of the animated TV series *Franklin*, produced by
Nelvana Limited, Neurones France s.a.r.l. and Neurones Luxembourg S.A.,
based on the Franklin books by Paulette Bourgeois and Brenda Clark.

Story written by Sharon Jennings.

Illustrated by Sean Jeffrey, Sasha McIntyre and Alice Sinkner.

Based on the TV episode *Gee Whiz, Franklin*, written by
Simon Racioppa and Richard Elliott.

 Kids Can Read is a trademark of Kids Can Press Ltd.

Franklin

Franklin is a trademark of Kids Can Press Ltd.
The character Franklin was created by Paulette Bourgeois and Brenda Clark.
Text © 2004 Contextx Inc.
Illustrations © 2004 Brenda Clark Illustrator Inc.

All rights reserved. No part of this publication may be reproduced, stored in a retrieval system or
transmitted, in any form or by any means, without the prior written permission of Kids Can Press
Ltd. or, in case of photocopying or other reprographic copying, a license from The Canadian
Copyright Licensing Agency (Access Copyright). For an Access Copyright license, visit
www.accesscopyright.ca or call toll free to 1-800-893-5777.

Kids Can Press acknowledges the financial support of the Government of Ontario, through the
Ontario Media Development Corporation's Ontario Book Initiative; the Ontario Arts Council; the
Canada Council for the Arts; and the Government of Canada, through the BPIDP, for our
publishing activity.

Published in Canada by
Kids Can Press Ltd.
29 Birch Avenue
Toronto, ON M4V 1E2

Published in the U.S. by
Kids Can Press Ltd.
2250 Military Róad
Tonawanda, NY 14150

www.kidscanpress.com

Series editor: Tara Walker
Edited by Jennifer Stokes
Designed by Céleste Gagnon

Printed in Hong Kong, China, by WKT Company Limited

The hardcover edition of this book is smyth sewn casebound.
The paperback edition of this book is limp sewn with a drawn-on cover.

CM 04 0 9 8 7 6 5 4 3 2 1
CM PA 04 0 9 8 7 6 5 4 3 2 1

National Library of Canada Cataloguing in Publication Data

Jennings, Sharon
   Franklin and the contest / Sharon Jennings ; illustrated by Sean Jeffrey, Sasha McIntyre,
Alice Sinkner.

(Kids Can read)
The character Franklin was created by Paulette Bourgeois and Brenda Clark.

ISBN 1-55337-491-6 (bound).   ISBN 1-55337-492-4 (pbk.)

I. Jeffrey, Sean II. McIntyre, Sasha III. Sinkner, Alice IV. Bourgeois, Paulette V. Clark, Brenda
VI. Title. VII. Series: Kids Can read (Toronto, Ont.)

PS8569.E563F7155 2004   jC813'.54   C2003-904250-2

Kids Can Press is a *lorus* ™ Entertainment company

Franklin and the Contest

Kids Can Press

Franklin can tie his shoes.

Franklin can count by twos.

And Franklin can do lots of

other things, too.

But Franklin cannot do something

for five hours without stopping.

This is a problem.

Franklin wants to win a contest.

One day, Franklin ran home from school.

He grabbed the mail.

There it was!

Gee Whiz Magazine:

The BEST Magazine for Kids!

"YIPPEE!" shouted Franklin.

Franklin sat down to read.

He read about
dinosaurs.

He read about
soccer players.

He read the riddle
page, and he read
the quiz page.

Then Franklin saw the contest page.

"Wow!" said Franklin.

Franklin called his friends.

He ran to meet them at the park.

"*Gee Whiz Magazine* is coming

to Woodland," said Franklin.

He told his friends about the contest.

"Wow!" said everybody.

"We can all enter," said Franklin.

"We have to do something

for five hours without stopping!"

Everybody wanted to enter

the contest.

"I can twiddle my thumbs

for five hours without

stopping," said Beaver.

"I can wiggle my ears,"

said Rabbit.

"I can hum," said Fox.

"I can eat blueberries and never, *ever* stop!" said Bear.

Everybody looked at Franklin.

"What can you do?" asked Beaver.

"I will think of something," he said.

Franklin went home to think.

First, he jumped

up and down.

In a minute he was tired.

Then, he stood
on his head.
In half a minute
he fell over.

Next, he rolled
around the yard.

In seconds he was dizzy.
"I will think some more later,"
said Franklin.

For supper, Franklin's mother

gave him fly soup.

"Yummy!" said Franklin.

"I *know* I can eat fly soup for five hours!"

Franklin ate fly soup for one hour.

Then he held his tummy and moaned.

"I will have to think

of something else," he said.

Soon, it was time for bed.

"Think, think, think," said Franklin.

"Why are you frowning?"

asked his mother.

"I'm not frowning," he said.

"I'm thinking."

The next day, and the next day,

and the day after that,

Franklin did lots of things.

He skipped rope.

He spun in a circle.

He mooed

like a cow,

and he clucked

like a chicken.

Franklin could *do* all those things,

but *not* for five hours without stopping.

On Saturday, Franklin woke up early.

"YIPPEE!" he shouted.

"*Gee Whiz Magazine* is coming

to Woodland *today!*"

Then he frowned.

"Think, think, think," he said.

"I need something to do for the contest!"

Franklin walked to the park.

"Think, think, think," he said.

Franklin stood in line to enter the contest.

"Think, think, think," he said.

He met Mr. Possum

from *Gee Whiz Magazine.*

"Why are you frowning?"

asked Mr. Possum.

"I'm not frowning," said Franklin.

"I'm thinking."

"Hey, everybody!" said Mr. Possum.

"Franklin is going to think

for five hours!"

Franklin's friends were surprised.

Franklin was surprised.

"Ready! Set! Go!" shouted Mr. Possum.

Franklin began to think.

Franklin kept thinking
when Beaver
stopped twiddling.

He kept thinking
when Rabbit
stopped wiggling.

He kept thinking
when Fox
stopped humming.

And he kept

thinking

when Bear

stopped eating.

"Think, Franklin, think!"

shouted his friends.

29

"And the winner is … Franklin!"

said Mr. Possum.

"Gee whiz, Franklin!" said his friends.

"You did it! You won!"

"What will you do with your

prize money, Franklin?" asked Bear.

"Hmmm," said Franklin.

"I'll have to think about it!"